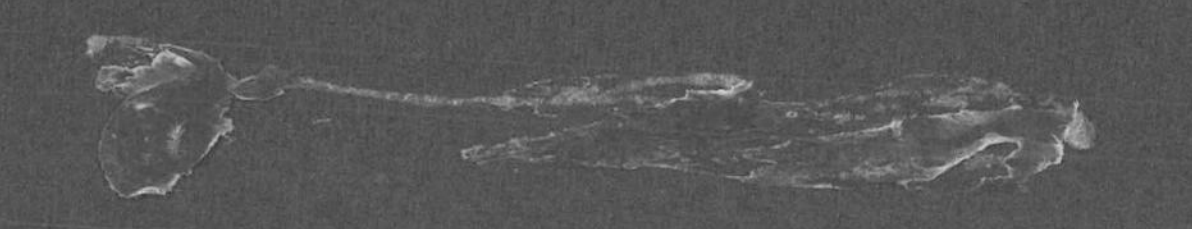

D0364667

Ferocious Wild Beasts!

For Tristan, Rhys and Stefan

FEROCIOUS WILD BEASTS
A JONATHAN CAPE BOOK 978 0 224 08352 2

Published in Great Britain by Jonathan Cape,
an imprint of Random House Children's Books
A Random House Group Company

This edition published 2009

3 5 7 9 10 8 6 4 2

RANDOM HOUSE CHILDREN'S BOOKS
61–63 Uxbridge Road, London W5 5SA

www.**kidsatrandomhouse**.co.uk
www.**rbooks**.co.uk

Addresses for companies within The Random House Group Limited can be found at:
www.randomhouse.co.uk/offices.htm

THE RANDOM HOUSE GROUP Limited Reg. No. 954009

A CIP catalogue record for this book is available from the British Library.

Printed in Singapore

FEROCIOUS WILD BEASTS!

Chris Wormell

A TOM MASCHLER BOOK
JONATHAN CAPE · LONDON

A bear was strolling in the forest
one day . . .

when he met a small boy,
sitting on a tree stump,
looking rather glum.

“What’s the matter?” asked the bear.

“I’m lost,” sniffed the boy, “and I’m in terrible trouble.”

“Dear me, why’s that?” enquired the bear.

“Because my mum said I must never go into the forest,” replied the boy, “but I did. And now I’m lost!”

“Don’t worry!” said the bear with a laugh. “I’ll soon show you the way out. The forest isn’t so bad, you know.”

“It is!” declared the boy. “My mum says the forest is full of *ferocious wild beasts*!”

"Really?" said the bear. "Is it? What are they like?"

"They're all hairy," replied the boy. "And they hide in the shadows and then they pounce on you and gobble you up!"

"Do they . . . er, do they gobble up bears too?" asked the bear, nervously.

"Of course," replied the boy. "They gobble up everything!"

The bear peered fearfully into the shadows between the trees. "I think we'd better go," he said.

They had not gone far when they met an elephant having a snack.

"Anyone for a banana?" asked the elephant.

"You'd better watch out, Elephant," advised the bear. "This young man tells me there are *ferocious wild beasts* on the loose!"

"Oh dear!" said the elephant, dropping his banana. "Are they *very* wild?"

"The wildest beasts ever!" said the boy. "They're SO big they could step on you and squish you just like that!"

"But, er . . . they couldn't squish an elephant, could they?" asked the elephant.

"Easily!" replied the boy.

“Oh crumbs!” gulped the elephant.

“You don’t mind if I tag along with you, do you?”

And soon all three were creeping through the forest.

Before long they met a lion sunbathing on a rock.
"Sit down and enjoy the sun!" said the lion with a flick of his tail.

"Not likely!" replied the bear. "Don't you know there are *ferocious wild beasts* about?"

"Are there?" gulped the lion. "How ferocious?"

"The most ferocious type of all," declared the boy. "And they have sharp claws and big teeth and can bite your head off in a second!"

"Yikes!" yelped the lion. "But they couldn't do that to a lion, could they?"

"I think they like eating
lions the best," replied the boy.
"Oh help!" whimpered the lion,
his mane all standing on end.
"You wouldn't mind if I came
along with you, would you?"

So off they went, tiptoeing through the forest.
And soon they met a crocodile . . .

And a wolf . . .

And a python.

Now the sun was sinking.
“The night-time is when the ferocious wild beasts
come out to hunt,” said the boy.

Just then they heard a sound . . .
like the sound of a terrible beast
stomping through the undergrowth.

Then they saw a light flickering through the tree trunks
like a great glowing eye . . .

And then they heard a wild roar echoing through the forest . . .

And they all ran for their lives!

Well, except for the small boy, who was the bravest. He crept forward and saw that it wasn't a ferocious wild beast at all – it was something *much* worse . . .

It was a
ferocious
wild mum!

"Jack! Jack!" she roared.
"Where are you, you naughty boy?"

"*There* you are," she sighed. "Didn't I tell you *never* to go into the forest? Didn't I tell you about all the ferocious wild beasts?"

“But, Mum,” Jack protested,
“I didn’t see any ferocious wild beasts.”